ELY PUBLIC LIBRARY
P.O. Box 249
1595 Dows St.
Ely, IA 52227

ASSASSIN

TONY BRADMAN

D1194942

With illustrations by
Martin Remphry

Barrington Stoke

To Leon Remphry

1046699

First published in 2007 in Great Britain by
Barrington Stoke Ltd
18 Walker Street, Edinburgh, EH3 7LP

www.barringtonstoke.co.uk

This edition first published 2011
Reprinted 2014, 2018

Copyright © 2007 Tony Bradman
Illustrations © 2007 Martin Remphry

The moral right of Tony Bradman and Martin Remphry to
be identified as the author and illustrator of this work has
been asserted in accordance with the Copyright, Designs and
Patents Act, 1988

All rights reserved. No part of this publication may be
reproduced in whole or in any part in any form without the
written permission of the publisher

A CIP catalogue record for this book is available
from the British Library upon request

ISBN: 978-1-84299-979-0

Printed in Great Britain by Charlesworth Press

ELY PUBLIC LIBRARY
P.O. Box 249
1595 Dows St.
Ely, IA 52227

Contents

1   Leader of the Pack   1

2   A Rich Purple Cloak   10

3   Into the Night   19

4   Silent Creeping   27

5   A Total Surprise   37

6   Going Home – In Style   45

     Hadrian's Wall: The Facts   55

Chapter 1
Leader of the Pack

The boy was running down the forest path. He was following the tracks that a wolf pack had left. Suddenly he stopped. He dropped to one knee and grinned.

"A wolf left the pack here, Father," the boy said. He was peering at the ground. You could see his breath in the cold air. "One set of tracks goes off that way ..." he began. He pointed into the forest. "But, look, the rest keep straight on."

1

"You're right, Owen," said the boy's father. His name was Madoc. Both of them had long hair tied back, and they were both wearing thick green tunics and trousers. Madoc looked at the tracks. "There's blood there, too," he said. "Well done, my son – you must have hit the wolf with your spear after all."

Owen's grin grew even bigger. The people of his tribe thought that killing a wolf was a great deed. Owen's tribe was the Votadini. They'd lived in the north of Britain for as long as anyone could remember. Their land was rich, and full of hills and forests. The Votadini were farmers, and they bred cattle and sheep.

But there were wolves in the woods. In winter the nights were full of the sound of their hungry howling – and they came sniffing round the sheep pens like grey ghosts. So the men of the tribe sat up in the dark hours to protect the flocks. And this year, for the first time, Owen had been with the men.

He thought again of the moment when he'd seen the wolves. He'd thrown his spear at them and raised the alarm. The wolves had run off.

Then, at first light, he and his father had set out to track them down.

"Come on, Father," said Owen and he jumped to his feet. "Let's go and finish the beast off. It can't have got very far if it's hurt, can it?"

"No, Owen, we're not doing that," said Madoc. He was walking along the path, looking down at the main set of tracks. "We follow the pack."

"Why, Father?" said Owen. He was angry. In his mind he could already see himself with his own wolf skin. The people of the village would be impressed. "Can't we just get this one now, then hunt the rest of them later?"

"But the wolf might be dead already," said Madoc. "Even if it isn't, it's not the leader. The one we need to kill is still out there, at the head of the pack."

"I don't understand," said Owen with a scowl. He hated it when his father talked to him as if he were a child, like his little sister Cadi.

"It's simple," said Madoc with a sigh. "Cut a man's head off, and his body is useless. Well, it's just the same with a wolf pack. Kill their leader and they don't know what to do, at least until a new leader takes over."

Owen scowled even more. He opened his mouth to answer back. But his father suddenly looked up, like a deer who senses a hunter nearby.

"Did you hear that?" Madoc whispered. "There it is again ..."

Owen's father was scowling himself now.
He put a finger to his lips. He stepped off
the path and nodded to Owen to follow him.
They crept between the trees. Soon they
were at the far edge of the forest and
peered out. Madoc made sure they stayed
hidden.

In front of them was a valley with a river running through it. Owen drew in his breath sharply. Just next to them, at the edge of the forest, was a warrior sitting on a pony. As they watched, the man gave a long, low whistle, and two more warriors came galloping up the slope towards him on their ponies.

"They're men of the Brigantes tribe. From the south," whispered Madoc.

Owen stared at his father. Did he think Owen was that stupid? Of course, he knew what tribe the warriors came from. He could tell from the pattern of the blue tattoos on their faces, and the shapes of their shields and spear blades. He knew the Brigantes' lands were right next to his own people's farms. And Owen knew that they were meant to stay there, on their side.

"What are they doing here, in our land?" he whispered back to his father.

"They look like advance scouts to me," Madoc said softly. He looked angry. "And you know who the Brigantes work for, don't you?"

Then Owen heard a new sound, a steady *tramp-tramp-tramp*. He felt the ground shake under his feet. Owen looked across the valley. What he saw was terrible. There was a long line of soldiers. They were marching over the hill, down the valley. The red crests of their helmets were nodding and the cold winter sunlight glinted off their shields and armour.

The Romans were coming!

Chapter 2
A Rich Purple Cloak

Madoc quickly pulled his son back,
deeper into the shadows under the trees.
But Owen couldn't take his eyes off the
Roman soldiers as they tramp-tramp-
tramped down the valley, with the
Brigantes scouts riding on ahead.

Owen knew all about the Romans, of
course. They had come to Britain many
summers ago, in the time of his

grandfather's grandfather. The Romans had fought and conquered all the weak tribes in the south of Britain. They had tried to defeat the Votadini too. That was when Owen's grandfather was young. The old people of the Votadini tribe still talked about those dark days.

The Romans had burnt many villages. They had killed the people or taken them off to be slaves. But the fierce Votadini had fought back, and at last the Romans had left them alone. After that, there had been peace for nearly forty summers. The Votadini even traded with the Romans now and the Romans often came north to buy the strong little ponies bred by the Votadini.

So Owen had seen Roman soldiers before. But he'd only seen them in small groups. The column tramping through the valley was like a great river, a torrent of men and weapons and armour. There were wagons pulled by mules too. The drivers were yelling and cracking whips over the poor animals' heads and the wagon wheels were enormous – crushing anything in their way.

Owen watched the Roman soldier who was riding a beautiful white horse at the front of the column. He had a tidy, clipped beard and a helmet with a tall red crest. He wore a golden breast-plate, and a rich purple cloak.

"This means war, doesn't it?" Owen whispered. "What can we do?"

Owen thought of his mother and Cadi. Their village had been burned once before – when his grandfather was young. Owen would give anything to make sure it wasn't burned again. He didn't want to think about his family being killed or made into slaves of the Romans.

"We can't do much here," said Madoc, his face full of fear. "But we can warn everyone. Come on, Owen – there's not a moment to lose!"

The village was nearly half a day's walk from the forest. Owen and his father had left at dawn to track the wolves. Now they ran all the way and got back quickly. All was peaceful. The round, thatched huts were still there, and people were getting ready to eat their evening meal.

Madoc and Owen ran straight to the Great Hall of Fintan. Fintan was the Chief of the village and Madoc told him what they had seen. Fintan frowned. He called for a meeting of the Tribal Council.

Later that evening the Great Hall was packed with warriors old and young. Their faces looked grim in the flickering torchlight.

"Madoc brings evil news," said Fintan. He shook his grey head. "I had hoped never to see a Roman army again. But my spies in the south had warned me the army was on its way to us. They said that the Emperor Hadrian himself has come to Britain to fight us once more."

The men in the Great Hall muttered together. They looked at each other. Their faces were frightened. Owen knew this was bad news. And suddenly he thought of the man he'd seen riding in front of the Roman soldiers. He must be the Emperor, the leader of the Romans.

"We should attack them as soon as we can," said a young warrior, his eyes glowing. "They'll make camp tonight, so we could strike at dawn."

"Well, I'm not sure we should attack them at all," said an older warrior with many scars. "Maybe we should just ask them what they want."

"We know that already," said the young warrior. "They want to take our land and make us their slaves. Look what they've done to the Brigantes!"

A great roar went up, and a huge argument began. Some men agreed with the young warrior, others with the older one. Owen listened. He tried to make sense of what he was hearing. But it was no good.

The argument went on for ages, until at last Fintan yelled for silence.

"This isn't getting us anywhere," he said. "Let's sleep on it, and decide what to do in the morning. I'll send messengers to the other free tribes. They too need to know the Romans are coming."

Slowly the warriors left the Great Hall. Their faces were grim and anxious. But Owen stood still. He'd just had a crazy thought.

What if he were to kill the leader of the pack? What if he killed the Emperor Hadrian himself?

Chapter 3
Into the Night

It was a terrific idea, Owen told himself. His father had said if you killed the leader of a wolf pack the others would be scared off. Would the same be true of a Roman army? Kill their leader, and they might be scared off too. Owen was sure it was worth a try, anyway.

For a moment he wanted to shout at everyone in the Great Hall to stop and

listen to him – he had the answer, and it
was so simple! But he was just a boy, and he
had a feeling they would take no notice.
Even if they did, Owen knew they wouldn't
let him do the job. The task would be given
to an adult – who'd also get all the glory,
of course

So Owen frowned and kept his mouth
shut. He made up his mind then and there
that he would save his family and his tribe,
and get all the glory ...

"Come on, Owen, don't just stand there dreaming," said his father. "Your mother will be waiting for us."

Owen followed his father to their hut. His family ate together. Owen's mother had made a hot barley broth. Owen could see his parents were worried. Even little Cadi didn't chatter about her day, or pester Owen to play with her. She seemed to know something was wrong.

"Come on, you two," said Owen's mother at last. "Time for bed."

Owen took off his thick outer tunic and shoes and lay down in the corner where he slept. He pulled the fur covers over him. He watched as his mother tucked Cadi in, and listened as she sang a low lullaby to her. They had the same colour hair, a deep red. The firelight made his mother's hair shine.

She came to Owen after a bit and laid a
warm hand on his cheek, and kissed him.
"Sleep well, my young warrior," she said,
just as she did every night. But now Owen
could see in her eyes the fear for him and
Cadi, and suddenly he felt cold all over.

Owen's father was standing behind her and looking down at Cadi. He turned to Owen and smiled, and then they went into their own sleeping place. There was a blanket hanging on a rope between their bed and the rest of the hut.

Owen had worked out what he was going to do. He lay still and waited till he was sure the others were asleep. It seemed to take ages. Cadi was soon breathing deeply, but Owen could hear his parents talking and talking … At last, the sound of deep breathing came from behind the blanket too.

Owen slowly slipped out from under his covers. He quickly pulled on his tunic and shoes. Then he inched towards the hut door, careful not to make any noise.

Suddenly he stopped. He'd need a weapon if he was going to kill the Roman Emperor – and not a hunting spear. A spear was too long and clumsy. He was going to have to do a lot of sneaking around and hiding, and then attack swiftly and silently from close up.

Owen knew what he needed. His father had just the thing. Madoc kept his weapons hanging near the door and Owen looked at them now. There was the ox-hide shield and the war spear with its blade in the shape of a leaf. He could see his father's beautiful sword and dagger. Their blades glinted in the low flames of the fire.

Owen took the dagger down and crept silently through the hut doorway.

It was cold outside, and all was still. But there was a full moon and its silver light cast deep shadows. Owen moved between the shadows and headed for the turf wall that went all round the village. He thought maybe there'd be extra guards tonight, and he soon saw he was right. There were four warriors beside the main gate, and three more up on the turf wall.

Owen crept along in the shadows. He had to find a way to get out. He didn't want anyone to see and then catch him before he'd even left the village. It would be just too shameful if he had to go back to his parents now.

But the warriors were all looking out into the distance beyond the village. They weren't worried about boys trying to slip away into the dark outside the village. At last Owen got his chance. He crept over the wall and no guards saw him. He dashed across a moonlit field and hid in some trees. He stopped there, his heart beating fast.

There was no going back. He was an assassin – a killer – with a job to do ...

Chapter 4
Silent Creeping

Owen nearly gave up and ran back to his parents when he saw the Roman camp. It was a huge square – bigger than his own village, with a ditch and a wall of earth. Inside it were hundreds of tents in straight lines.

He saw now that the power of the Romans was awesome. They had made this camp in one night, and there were thousands of them here. How could he, a

boy on his own, kill the Emperor? He didn't even know if he could get inside the camp. There were four gate-ways, one on each side of the camp, but they were all well lit with torches. Each one had four soldiers to guard it.

But Owen knew that he had to try. He made himself calm down and look at the camp slowly. And at last he saw what he needed. Near one corner there was a clump of bushes which would give him some cover ...

A few moments later he crept silently between the tents. He used the skills he'd learned when he was on the hunting trail with his father. No one saw him. He made for the middle of the camp. That was where the Emperor would be. Most of the soldiers were snoring in their tents with their weapons stacked outside. But a few were awake. They were playing dice or just talking. They were talking in Latin, of course, and Owen couldn't understand a word.

At last he saw a big tent, one that looked more important than the others. Two guards stood at the entrance, one on either side. They each held a spear and the sharp points glinted in the leaping flames of a torch.

Owen ducked down and crept round behind the tent. He ran his hands over it, but couldn't find any gaps. What if there were guards inside? He needed to look inside the tent before he found a way in. He had to make sure he had the right place and that the Emperor was on his own.

Owen cut a small hole with his father's dagger and peered in. It was hard to see anything at first. The only light came from two small oil lamps on a low table inside. But bit by bit Owen's eyes got used to the dark. There was another table, covered with rolled-up papers, a stand with a golden breast-plate and a red-crested helmet hanging from it.

And then Owen saw him – the man with the clipped beard who'd been at the front of the Roman army.

Now he was lying on a low couch with a thick bearskin over him to keep out the cold. His eyes were shut in sleep. But it was definitely him.

And he had to be Hadrian. Who else would have a tent this size to himself, and guards? Owen was surprised he only had two guards. *How big-headed these Romans were*, he thought and anger flooded through him. They must have thought they were so powerful they didn't have to worry about their leader being attacked.

Well, it was time they learned that they couldn't push the Votadini around. Owen pushed the dagger back into the hole he'd made and cut right down to the ground. Then he slipped inside.

He stood still for a moment. His heart was hammering in his chest. The entrance to the tent was covered, so the guards couldn't see him. He crept over to the couch and stood beside the sleeping Roman. The hilt of the dagger felt slippery, Owen's palm was wet with sweat. He wiped his hand on his tunic, then lifted the dagger slowly, ready to strike.

A moment passed. Owen was shaking from head to foot. Could he do it? He'd killed lots of animals, of course – fish and forest birds and rabbits for the pot – but killing a man was, well ... very different.

Owen frowned and gritted his teeth. A picture of Cadi asleep at home popped into his mind, and he knew he *had* to do it, to protect her. He pulled his arm back to give the blow as much force as possible ...

And then he struck. But suddenly Hadrian's eyes flew open.

He quickly rolled aside, and Owen felt the dagger slam into the couch. The Roman yelled, and threw himself at Owen. The two of them crashed to the rug on the floor of the tent. Owen tried to wriggle free, but the Roman had him pinned down and was shouting at the top of his voice.

The guards rushed in and grabbed Owen. They dragged him away from the Emperor and made the boy kneel. One guard held him from behind, while the other whipped out a sword and held it to Owen's throat.

Owen closed his eyes, sure he was about to die.

Chapter 5
A Total Surprise

Owen felt the cold, sharp metal of the guard's sword press into the soft skin of his throat. Then he heard a deep voice saying something, and the blade was suddenly gone. Owen opened his eyes and looked up.

The man he'd tried to kill was standing in front of him. He was wearing a short tunic, and his legs were bare. He was looking down at Owen, a frown on his face. The man didn't seem to notice the other guards who came rushing into the tent, swords drawn. One threw a cloak over the Emperor's back, the rich purple cloak Owen had seen before.

The Emperor said something to Owen. It sounded as if he was asking a question, but Owen didn't understand. He didn't answer. The guard who'd held a sword to his throat was angry. He yelled at Owen and lifted his hand to hit him. Owen waited for the blow to fall, but the Emperor spoke again. His voice was hard and cross, and the guard stood still.

Then the Emperor muttered something to another of the guards. This one ran out of the tent and came back moments later with one of the scouts Owen and his father had seen at the edge of the forest.

The Emperor spoke to the scout, and the scout turned to Owen.

"Who are you, child?" said the scout. He talked in Owen's own Celtic language. "And why did your tribe send a boy to try and kill the Emperor Hadrian? I know you're from the Votadini. Why would Fintan do such a stupid thing?"

"I am Owen, son of Madoc," Owen said proudly, his head held high. "No one sent me, not Fintan or anyone else. It was my idea, mine alone."

The man told the Emperor what Owen had said. Hadrian frowned, then spoke again.

"So why did you want to kill the Emperor?" said the scout.

"I wanted to save my people," said Owen with a shrug. "I thought that if I killed their Emperor, then the Romans wouldn't invade our lands."

"You're lucky you didn't succeed," said
the scout. "You'd just have made them
angry. They're not coming to invade your
lands anyway."

"What ... what do you mean?" said Owen. He didn't understand. But the scout was talking to Hadrian, and didn't answer. The Emperor listened to what the scout said. He kept his eyes fixed on Owen. At last his frown vanished and he began to look thoughtful.

Hadrian seemed to make up his mind what to do. He barked some orders in that deep, strong voice of his, and most of the guards left the tent. Only the two guards from the tent stayed there, with the scout and the Emperor himself. The guards pulled Owen up to his feet.

"You're a lucky boy," said the scout. "I think you're going to get away with it. The Emperor wants to explain things to you. He'll talk and I'll tell you what he says."

Now it was Owen's turn to listen – and what he heard came as a total surprise to him. Hadrian talked about why his army was in the north of Britain. They were there to build a great wall of stone right across Britain, from one side to the other.

Hadrian showed Owen the papers on the table. Owen had never seen anything like them before. Hadrian said they were plans of the wall, pictures of what it would be like. There were also things called maps, simple plans of lands. Hadrian showed Owen the map of the Roman Empire. Britain was a tiny place in the corner.

"I get it," Owen muttered. "You're making a wall to keep the tribes of the south in, and keep us out. Just like we keep the wolves out of our sheep pens."

"You could think of it like that," said Hadrian, with a smile. "But it's a wall to keep us Romans in as well. Our empire is too big. I'm drawing a line here that says –

we'll go this far, and no further. It means that even the emperors who come after me won't invade your lands. My wall will make sure that your people stay free forever. But," said Hadrian, "I might not be able to build my wall unless you help me, Owen, son of Madoc."

Owen looked at the Emperor. Suddenly he felt that this was a man he could trust. Even if he was a Roman, and an Emperor with an enormous army.

But how could a boy like him help the great Roman Emperor?

"All right," said Owen. "What is it that you want me to do?"

Chapter 6
Going Home – In Style

"This is my worry," said Hadrian. "Your people – and the other free tribes – could make it very difficult for us to build the wall. I need someone to take a message for me. I want you to go home and tell your chief that I'm here to talk. That I don't want to invade your country."

"But I'm just a boy," said Owen. "My chief won't listen to me."

"Oh, you're more than just a boy," said Hadrian. "There aren't many men who could sneak into a Roman camp and almost kill an Emperor. That takes a lot of courage … But I do need to talk to the captain of my guards about how easy it was to get past them."

Hadrian turned to frown at the two sentries. They both blushed and snapped to attention at once. The scout grinned. But Owen took no notice. He was still thinking about what Hadrian had said.

"I'm not sure," Owen muttered at last. "You don't know Fintan and the other grown-ups in my village. They don't even listen to each other."

"Very well," said the Emperor. He smiled suddenly. "I'll send you back to your village. The people there will never forget the way you come back."

Then the great Emperor Hadrian started barking orders again ...

And that's how it happened. The next morning, Owen rode back to his village on the Emperor's beautiful white horse. Behind him rode the three scouts, and behind them marched a squad of Roman soldiers. They were carrying boxes – gifts from Hadrian to Owen's people.

Owen could see that his people were watching. There were warriors at the village entrance, and more lined up on the turf wall. All of them were ready to fight. But Owen saw his father point at him, and say something to old Fintan. The chief lifted his arm high, and the men put down their spears.

"Hello, Father," said Owen. He jumped off the Emperor's horse and ran up to the gate. Madoc was staring at him now with a strange look on his face – a mixture of amazement and anger. Owen grinned at him.

"Where have you been?" Madoc growled. "Your mother has been frantic with worry … and what are you doing with these Romans?"

"I'm sorry I ran off, Father," said Owen. "But I can explain everything. I've met the

Emperor, and he's sent me home with a message for Fintan."

There were snorts of laughter from the warriors, and Madoc scowled. "Don't talk nonsense, boy," snapped Madoc. "You're dreaming again."

"It's not nonsense," said the scout. "He speaks the truth, and you should be proud of him. He is as brave as any warrior. The great Emperor sent us and these soldiers with him."

The warriors whispered together. Madoc looked back at Owen. Fintan stepped forward and put his hand on Owen's arm.

"Well then, I'd better hear this message," said Fintan. "Come to the hall, Owen, and give it to me. The soldiers and the scouts can come with you."

Owen gave Fintan the message. Fintan sat in his hall. All round the hall stood the great men of the tribe and all of them listened to what Owen had to say. An argument broke out as soon as Owen finished, but Fintan shouted and held his hand up.

"Thank you for this, Owen," he said. "I will talk to the Emperor, and find out more about his great wall – the wall that will keep the Votadini free."

Later that same day, Owen went back to the Roman camp with a reply from the old chief. And Hadrian grinned when he heard it.

There were many days of talking between Hadrian and Fintan, and the chiefs of the other free tribes. At first they didn't trust the Roman Emperor and his army. But slowly they saw he meant what he said. Owen was always at Hadrian's right hand. Even his parents forgave him for what he'd done.

In the spring of that year, Hadrian's army started building the wall.

The wall's still there today – it's called Hadrian's Wall. By the time it was finished, many summers later, Cadi was a grown-up woman, and Owen was a man with a wife and a son of his own. He had plenty of sheep, and he was a skilful hunter, too, a man whose hut was full of wolf skins.

But he was always known as Owen, son of Madoc – The Boy Who Could Have Killed The Roman Emperor, And Lived To Tell The Tale!

HADRIAN'S WALL: THE FACTS

Owen isn't real. He's not in the history books. But someone like him could have lived. Roman writers talk about the Votadini tribe. Their lands were in south-eastern Scotland, from Edinburgh to Northumberland. They spoke a Celtic language - a bit like modern Welsh - and they were warriors, hunters and farmers!

There were lots of other tribes in Roman Britain. Roman history books talk about the Brigantes. They lived in the lands that are Northumberland today. When the Romans first invaded Britain, the queen of the **Brigantes** was **Cartimandua**. The chief of another tribe in the south of Britain was called **Caractacus**. He fought the Romans but lost. So he fled to Cartimandua. He wanted her to help him but she handed him over to the Romans. After that the Brigantes were friends of the Romans.

The **Iceni** were another famous tribe. They lived in the area we call Norfolk now. They were famous for being good warriors and breeding fine horses. In 60 AD their king died and the Romans tried to take over their kingdom. But the king of the Iceni had a powerful wife, a tough warrior queen called **Boudica**. She rebelled. She took an enormous army to fight against the Romans. She burned down three Roman towns - Colchester, London and St Albans - and killed 80,000 people.

But in the end the Romans defeated
and killed her. You can see her statue
in London – on Westminster Bridge.

The Celts were farmers, but they were warriors, too. They loved beautiful weapons – their swords and shields were decorated with lots of patterns made up of flowing lines. The richest warriors fought in chariots. They would charge the enemy, and then get down from the chariots to fight on foot. Celtic warriors were head hunters. They liked to cut off the heads of their dead enemies and keep them as prizes. Sometimes they hung the heads from their belts.

The Celts worshipped lots of gods and goddesses. There were important ones like **Lug** and **Epona**, the horse goddess, but there were lots of less important ones too - local gods and spirits. Celtic priests were called **Druids**. Historians think that they killed humans for sacrifices. The Romans weren't keen on the Druids, and they attacked their special place on the island of Anglesey in North Wales.

Hadrian is definitely real. He was born in 76 AD and became Emperor of Rome in 117 AD. He died in 138 AD. Most Roman Emperors stayed at home in Rome but Hadrian enjoyed travelling. He visited Britain in 122 AD. That's when he decided to build his famous wall. His reason was to stop the Roman empire getting any bigger. And he did have a tidy, clipped beard -

you can see it in the statues of him and on the coins that have his picture.

He liked building. He had an enormous villa in Rome, and he put up lots of other buildings. He built new cities too.

Before Hadrian there were some mad, bad Emperors. **Caligula** was an Emperor who was totally mad. He made his horse into a senator, a member of the government.

He told his soldiers to attack the sea because he didn't like **Neptune,** the Roman god of the sea. Caligula had lots of people killed and in the end he was killed. Hadrian was much wiser and people sometimes say that the Roman Empire was at its best and strongest when he was emperor.

Hadrian's Wall is **74 miles** long. It runs from one coast of Britain to the other. It starts at Bowness on the Cumbrian coast and finishes at somewhere called **Wallsend** in Newcastle upon Tyne. The wall was five metres high and three metres thick. It took six years to build. It had **16** big forts, **79** smaller forts called milecastles, and lots of turrets. Hadrian also built another wall, on the border with Germany, but nothing of that is left today.

We think Hadrian's soldiers did build the wall. The Roman army's job was to fight. But the soldiers had to do other things too, just like in a modern army. The Roman army had lots of experts in its ranks - engineers, and builders of all kinds. And they always built a camp when they stopped for the night - most of all when they were in enemy lands!

The first Roman to come to Britain was Julius Caesar. He invaded with his army twice. First in 55 and then in 54 BC. But he didn't stay. Then in 43 AD the Emperor Claudius sent an army. This time the Romans defeated the Britons and started to invade all of Britain. But it was only 40 years later that the Roman army got as far as the lands of the Votadini!

Our books are tested
for children and young people by
children and young people.

Thanks to everyone who consulted on
a manuscript for their time and effort in
helping us to make our books better
for our readers.

More **horrid history**
from Barrington Stoke ...

Harald Hardnut
TONY BRADMAN

The Vikings are raiders and plunderers, sailors and warriors. Everywhere they go, people flee in fear.

But the toughest Viking of them all is Harald Hardnut. Harald wants power, land and riches. There's no prize too great or battle too tough.

Does anyone dare stand in his way?

War Games
TERRY DEARY

George is an evacuee from the Blitz. He has no friends and no family to turn to. At least he has cricket.

Esther is a Jewish girl in Nazi Germany. All her freedoms have been taken away. She cannot even play football.

Can a love of sport give two young people a way to survive?

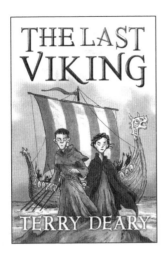

The Last Viking
TERRY DEARY

When Emma sees Viking ships sailing towards her home, she races to sound the alarm. The monks must hide their gold. Run for their lives.

But no one will listen. They say the Vikings are long gone. Can Emma and her brother Symeon save their village – and their country – from betrayal and attack?

Dick Turpin: Legends and Lies
TERRY DEARY

Today is the day Dick Turpin will die. A young boy waits in the crowd below the scaffold. Waits to see him hang.

In the crowd are five people. For some of them, the highwayman is a hero. For some of them, he is a monster.

Who is telling the truth?

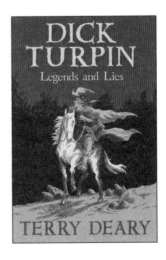

www.barringtonstoke.co.uk